Thanks to our contributors! All your responses helped inspire and inform this book (even if you don't see your <u>exact</u> response here). Leah Thaxton, Natasha and Louise Brown, Alice Swan and Emlyn Simmonds, Naomi Colthurst, Hannah Love, Susan Holmes, Emma Eldridge, Kim Lund, David Woodhouse, Mohammed Kasim, Donna and Robin Payne, Miles Poynton, Lizzie Bishop, Helen Hughes and family, Kate Ward, Sam Brown, The Gates family, Niriksha Bharadia, Louise, Ariella, Charlie, Jasmyn, Ruth Atkins, Josh, Connor, Catherine and Cleo, Jemima and Harley, Sarah Stoll and family, Pedro and Otto Nelson, Dinah Wood and family, Anna and Ella-Grace, Laurence, Finnegan, Nancy, George, The Goodey family, Amy, Michelle, Katie, Danny, Grace and Isla, Paul and Ezra, Dexter and Saffron, Gemma and Liyana, Freda and Tobias, Pall, Hannah, Faye, Fleur, Emma, Rebecca, Derya, Rebecca, Catherine, Tina, Angee, Phil, Nicola, Iona, Joanne, Kylie, Louise, Lydia, Noreen, Jane, Laura, Kayleigh, Ruth, Marion, Claire and Chris.

This Faber book belongs to:

I LIKE **BEES**, I don't like honey!

I like butterflies! I don't like sitting down because my bottom goes FLAT.

I like **chatting**. Let me tell you about this book . . . A minimum of 5% of the publisher's net revenue from the sale of any copy is payable to the NSPCC. First published in the UK in 2017 by Faber and Faber Ltd, Bloomsbury House, 74-77 Great Russell Street, London WC1B 3DA Printed in Malta. All rights reserved. Text © Faber and Faber, 2017 Illustrations © Fiona Lumbers, 2017 The moral rights of Fiona Lumbers have been asserted. A CIP record for this book is available from the British Library. ISBN 978-0-571-33419-3 10 9 8 7 6 5 4 3 2 1

Written by Sam Bishop

Inspired by lots of children and their parents!

Illustrated by Fiona Lumbers

ff

FABER & FABER

I'll tell you something that's a little bit **funny!**

Jackson likes bees but he doesn't like honey.

Aisha likes **playing outside,** even when it's cold.

But **Ben** likes playing **inside,** and sitting good as gold!

Mei likes painting and making a mess,
She doesn't like washing up
                              – or wearing a dress!

Tom likes space rockets and zooming through the sky! He doesn't like being told off, it makes him want to cry.

Skyler likes bouncing,
as high as she can go!

Noah likes his dad. He hates the word NO.

James likes paper aeroplanes!
They're his favourite toys.
Kai doesn't like strangers
or making lots of noise.

What do you **like**?
What **don't** you like?

Sam loves building things and following instructions.

He also loves **reading** but doesn't like **interruptions!**

Isla likes jellyfish, Mirai likes slides.
They both like climbing but they don't like bike rides!

Kobe likes dogs and the
funny things they do.
He doesn't like getting scratched
or picking up their poo!

Ava likes make-believe.
It really makes her laugh!
George doesn't like ketchup
or getting in the bath.

Jack likes **numbers** and sucking his thumb.

Tess likes her imaginary friend.
She loves chatting with her mum.

Everyone is different!
This much is true.
What you like, and what you don't,
it's really up to you!